My "s" Sound Box®

(The "sh" sound is included in this book along with blends.)

Library of Congress Cataloging-in-Publication Data
Moncure, Jane Belk.
My "s" sound box / by Jane Belk Moncure; illustrated by Colin King.
p. cm.
Summary: A little boy fills his sound box with many words that begin with the letter "s."
ISBN 1-56766-785-6 (lib. reinforced : alk. paper)
[1. Alphabet.] I. King, Colin, ill. II. Title.
PZ7.M739 Mys   2000
[E]—dc21   99-056568

My "s" Sound Box

Jane Belk Moncure

illustrated by Colin King

The Child's World

Little  had a box.

"I will find things that begin with my 's' sound," he said.

"I will put them into
my sound  box."

Little  took off his shoes,

his socks,

his sweater,

and his shirt.

Did he put the shoes, socks, sweater, and shirt into his box? He did.

Little  S put on his swimsuit

and his sandals

and went for a walk

on the sand.

He found a shovel 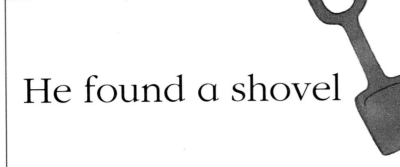 and a sand pail.

He made a sand castle.

Then he put the shovel,
the sand pail, and
the sand castle into his  box.

Little S went for a swim in the sea.

He saw a seal

swimming in the sea.

He saw six more seals on the sand.
Did he put seven seals into his box?

He did.

Little **S** found seashells all over the sand.

He also found a  starfish.

Did he put the seashells
and the starfish into his box?

He did.

Then he saw a  shark.

It was a small shark. So Little slipped it into a sack.

He put the sack into the box.

Then Little  saw a sea snake.

It was a small sea snake,
so he slipped it into the sack.

He put the sack back
into the box.

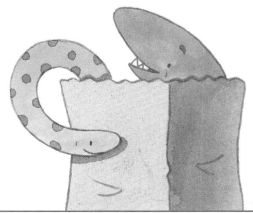

Later, Little  met a sailor.

The sailor gave him a

 sailor hat.

"Let's play," said the sailor.

They played on the

seesaw.

They slid down the slide.

Then they swung on the swings.

Suddenly, there was a big, noisy sound!

The sound was coming from the box.

"What is in the box?" asked the sailor.

"Things that begin with my 's' sound," said Little S.

"I sail on things that begin with your sound," said the sailor. "I sail on a

ship."

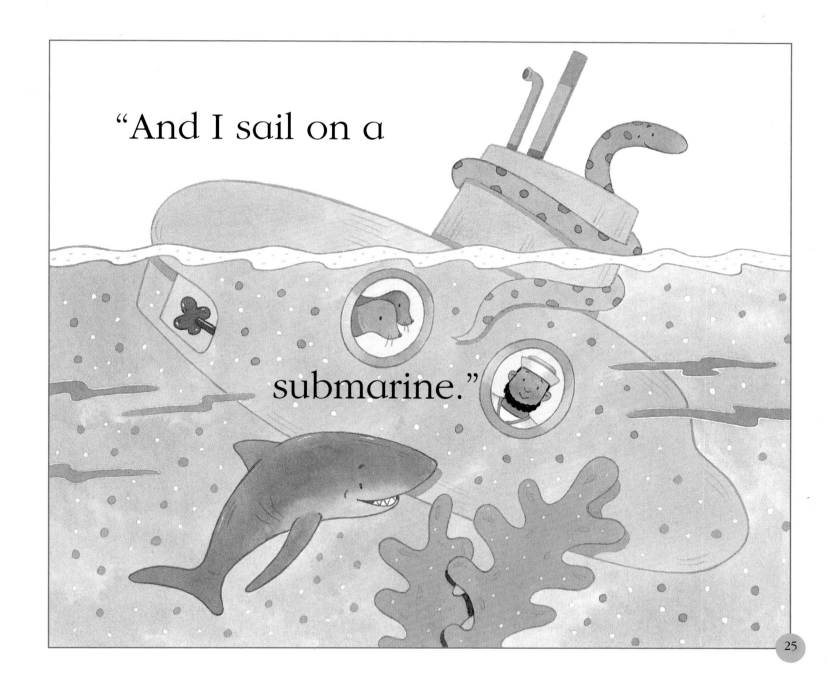

"And I sail on a

submarine."

The sailor helped Little 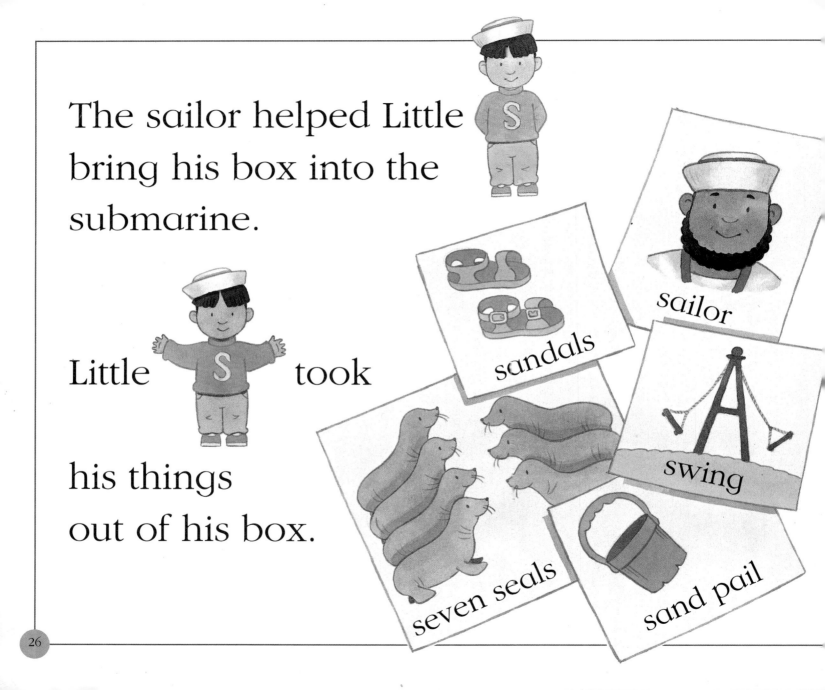 bring his box into the submarine.

Little took

his things
out of his box.

sandals

sailor

swing

seven seals

sand pail

26

And the sailor drew pictures of the ship, swing, slide, and seesaw.

sack

slide

starfish

sailor hat

seesaw

seashells

swimsuit

shark

sand castle

socks

sea snake

sweater

Can you read these words
with Little  ?

sunflower

stick

snail

sink

soap

salad

star

seed

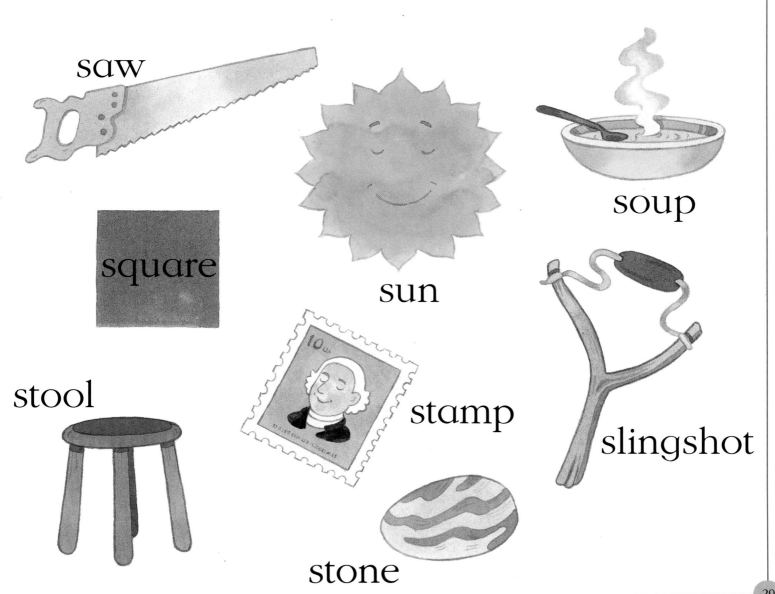

saw

soup

square

sun

stool

stamp

slingshot

stone

ABOUT THE AUTHOR AND ILLUSTRATOR

Jane Belk Moncure began her writing career when she was in kindergarten. She has never stopped writing. Many of her children's stories and poems have been published, to the delight of young readers, including her son Jim, whose childhood experiences found their way into many of her books.

Mrs. Moncure's writing is based upon an active career in early childhood education. A recipient of an M.A. degree from Columbia University, Mrs. Moncure has taught and directed nursery, kindergarten, and primary grade programs in California, New York, Virginia, and North Carolina. As a former member of the faculties of Virginia Commonwealth University and the University of Richmond, she taught prospective teachers in early childhood education.

Mrs. Moncure has travelled extensively abroad, studying early childhood programs in the United Kingdom, The Netherlands, and Switzerland. She was the first president of the Virginia Association for Early Childhood Education and received its award for outstanding service to young children.

A resident of North Carolina, Mrs. Moncure is currently a full-time writer and educational consultant. She is married to Dr. James A. Moncure, former vice president of Elon College.

Colin King studied at the Royal College of Art, London. He started his freelance career as an illustrator, working for magazines and advertising agencies.

He began drawing pictures for children's books in 1976 and has illustrated over sixty titles to date.

Included in a wide variety of subjects are a best-selling children's encyclopedia and books about spies and detectives.

His books have been translated into several languages, including Japanese and Hebrew. He has four grown-up children and lives in Suffolk, England, with his wife, three dogs, and a cat.